For Andy, Zachary, and Pat—
the best sand castle builders ever —N.Z.

To Leta, for all your love and compassion —M.V.

Text copyright © 2018 by Natalie Ziarnik
Jacket art and interior illustrations copyright © 2018 by Madeline Valentine

All rights reserved. Published in the United States by Schwartz & Wade Books,
an imprint of Random House Children's Books, a division of Penguin Random House LLC, New York.

Schwartz & Wade Books and the colophon are trademarks of Penguin Random House LLC.

Visit us on the Web! rhcbooks.com

Educators and librarians, for a variety of teaching tools, visit us at RHTeachersLibrarians.com

Library of Congress Cataloging-in-Publication Data is available upon request.
ISBN 978-1-101-93552-1 (hc) — ISBN 978-1-101-93553-8 (lib. bdg.) — ISBN 978-1-101-93554-5 (ebook)

The text of this book is set in Brandon Grotesque.
The illustrations for this book were done in goauche and digitally composed.
Book design by Rachael Cole

MANUFACTURED IN CHINA
2 4 6 8 10 9 7 5 3 1
First Edition

A LULLABY
of SUMMER
THINGS

Natalie Ziarnik &
Madeline Valentine

schwartz & wade books · new york

In the twilight blue
a porch light blinks.
An upper window winks.

A screen door sings

a lullaby of summer things.

Buckets tumbling.
Shovels jumbling.

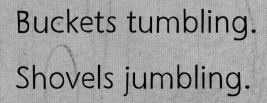

Bare feet skipping.

Wet towels dripping.

And you remember the beach that day—

the sea so cool,
the waves at play.

A clock chimes eight.

Dad shuts the gate.

Old floorboards rattle;
then stair steps tattle.

Spots run and hide.

A closet opens wide.

Red slippers sneak.

Two bright eyes peek.

And you remember the beach that day—

the sea so cool,

big paws at play.

Faucet hissing.

Washcloth missing.

Bubbles giggling.

Noses wiggling.

A toy boat tips.

Duck floats, then dips.

And you remember the beach that day—

the sea so cool,

sails far away.

A night-light glows.

A shadow grows.

A seashell roars.

A puppy snores.

Blown kisses hover
in the air and under cover.

Outside, squirrels sleep.

Distant cars beep-beep.

Poppies close.

Moonflowers pose.

And you remember the beach that day—

begging, begging,

"Can't we stay?"

A cricket strums.

Downstairs, Mama hums.

In the dusky evening light
a sleepy house says goodnight.

A half-moon listens.

One star glistens.

Ocean breezes sigh
your favorite summer lullaby.